ONE DAY WITH
MILO THE MONKEY
THE BANANA BONANZA

ONE DAY WITH YOUR FAVOURITE ANIMAL CHARACTER SERIES 1
BOOK 2

WISE WHIMSY

ONE DAY WITH MILO THE MONKEY

The Banana Bonanza

WISE WHIMSY

YOUNG MINDS PUBLISHING

CHAPTER 1:
THE GRAND PLAN

Once upon a time, in a lush jungle brimming with life, there lived a mischievous little monkey named Milo. This wasn't just any day for Milo; it was the day he'd been planning all week, the day of the Grand Banana Bonanza!

Milo's eyes sparkled with mischief as he scampered down the trunk of his favorite tree, his little heart filled with excitement. "Today's the day I feast on bananas till my belly's full!" he declared to a chorus of chirps and chatters from his jungle friends.

With a map sketched in the soft earth and a stick for pointing, Milo outlined his grand plan to himself. "First, I'll swing over to the banana grove by the waterfall. Then, I'll sneak past Louie the Lazy Leopard. And lastly, I'll grab the bananas from Benny the Bear's backyard," he plotted with a giggle, unaware that his sneaky plan would soon teach him a big lesson.

Off Milo went, his tiny feet barely touching the ground as he raced to the grove. He could almost taste the sweet bananas as he pictured them piled high, just waiting for him. "Mmm, banana sandwiches, banana muffins, banana everything!" he drooled.

But as he filled his little makeshift sack with the golden treasures, he didn't notice the pair of eyes watching him from behind the leaves. It was Louie the Leopard, intrigued by Milo's boldness. And as Milo dashed off with his loot, a banana fell from his sack, and with a slip and a trip, his plan began to unravel.

As the sun climbed higher in the sky, Milo's adventures were just beginning. But with each step, he was about to learn that every banana stolen and every rule broken comes with a price.

And so, with a sack full of bananas and a head full of dreams, Milo's grand plan was set into motion. Little did he know that by the end of the day, he would learn a lesson more valuable than all the bananas in the jungle.

CHAPTER 2:
BANANA BLITZ

Milo, with his tiny heart thumping with delight, continued his grand banana blitz. He had managed to gather bananas from the grove by the waterfall and now was on his way to the second part of his plan—Louie the Lazy Leopard's territory.

With his sack slung over his shoulder, heavy with bananas, he tiptoed past Louie, who was dozing under a canopy of thick leaves. "Easy peasy, lemon squeezy," Milo whispered to himself, a cheeky grin spreading across his face. He was so pleased with himself that he didn't notice Louie's ear twitch at the sound of his voice.

As he made his way through the jungle, Milo couldn't help but perform a little victory dance. He shimmied and shook, causing a banana to tumble out of his sack. It landed with a soft 'plop' near Louie's nose. Milo froze, his eyes wide with panic, but Louie just snuffled in his sleep and rolled over. Milo let out a sigh of relief and scooted away as fast as his little legs would carry him.

Next was Benny the Bear's backyard, a place where the juiciest bananas grew. Benny was busy fishing by the river, and Milo saw his chance. He darted in and out, swiping bananas with such speed that he became a blur of fur and mischief. He didn't stop to think that maybe Benny was saving those bananas for a special treat, or that taking without asking was not the kindest deed.

With his sack now bursting at the seams, Milo perched atop a high branch, gazing at his banana bounty. He was so engrossed in his triumph that he failed to hear the grumbles and murmurs of discontent from the other animals. They had all watched Milo's antics, and they were not amused by the little monkey's selfish spree.

As Milo sat munching on a particularly plump banana, he didn't realize that his actions were about to catch up with him. The jungle was watching, and the jungle was not happy. Milo was about to learn that for every action, there is a reaction, and not all reactions are as sweet as a ripe banana.

CHAPTER 3:
SLIPPERY CONSEQUENCES

Milo's day of mischief had taken a turn; it was now an afternoon of mishaps. With his sack now too full, he struggled to maintain his grip as he swung back towards his secret hideout. But Milo was about to learn that in the jungle, not everything goes as planned, especially when you're carrying a sack overflowing with stolen bananas.

As he maneuvered through the branches, a single banana slipped from the top of the pile and fell to the forest floor with a splat. Then, like a row of dominoes, one after another, bananas began to drop, leaving a trail behind him.

It was not long before Milo himself met the same fate as his bananas. Swinging with a bit too much confidence, he stepped on one of the fallen bananas. His feet flew out from under him, and with a comical 'whoa,' he went tumbling through the leaves, landing with a thud that sent birds flying from the treetops.

Dazed and covered in banana mush, Milo sat up. The jungle had grown quiet, and he felt dozens of eyes on him. There was Louie, looking miffed about being woken from his nap. There was Benny, holding an empty fishing net, his disappointment clear. And there were all the other animals, their looks of disapproval piercing Milo's heart.

Milo's ears drooped, and his smile faded. The laughter and thrills from his banana blitz seemed a distant memory now, replaced by the sinking feeling of guilt. He realized, perhaps for the first time, that his actions had consequences—not just for him, but for everyone around him.

As the reality of the situation settled in, Milo knew he had to make things right. But how? He was just one small monkey against a jungle of troubles he'd caused. It was a puzzle, but Milo loved puzzles, and he was determined to solve this one.

This chapter would be a turning point for Milo, a moment of self-reflection and realization. The slapstick humor of his fall is balanced with the emotional weight of his realization, showing young readers that it's okay to make mistakes as long as you learn from them. The language remains simple and engaging, with a focus on the visual comedy of the situation, while also beginning to introduce the concept of accountability.

CHAPTER 4:
LESSONS IN THE LEAVES

Milo sat amidst the banana chaos, his little heart heavy with regret. The jungle seemed to close in around him, a once friendly place now filled with the echoes of his thoughtlessness. As he pondered his next move, a voice called out to him, gentle and wise.

"Looks like you've got yourself in quite a pickle, Milo," said Geraldine the Giraffe, her long neck bending down to meet Milo's gaze. "But don't worry, every problem has a solution."

Milo looked up at Geraldine, his eyes brimming with tears. "But I didn't mean to," he sniffled. "I just wanted to have fun."

Geraldine smiled kindly. "Fun is wonderful, but it's even better when shared," she said. "Let me tell you a story."

And so, Geraldine told Milo about the time she ate too many leaves from the top of the trees, not leaving enough for the other animals who couldn't reach high. She learned that sharing was more important than having all the fun— or all the leaves—to herself.

Milo listened intently, his furry brow furrowed in thought. One by one, other animals came and shared their stories too. Benny the Bear talked about a time when he caught too many fish, leaving none for others and how lonely he felt eating them all by himself. Louie the Leopard shared how his napping once blocked the path and caused trouble for others.

With each story, Milo's understanding grew. He realized that he wasn't alone in making mistakes; what mattered was learning from them. He began to see that being part of the jungle meant looking out for each other. It was a lesson of balance, of give and take, of being a good friend and neighbor.

By the time the stories ended, Milo knew what he had to do. "I'm going to fix this," he declared, his voice steady and sure. "I will make things right."

CHAPTER 5:
A NEW DAY

The sun was beginning to dip below the treetops, casting a golden glow over the jungle as Milo set about making amends. He started by picking up all the bananas scattered on the ground, placing them back onto his leafy sled. But this time, it wasn't to hoard them for himself; it was to share them with everyone.

Milo went to Louie first, offering a bunch of bananas as an apology for disturbing his nap. Louie's grumpy face softened into a smile, and he accepted Milo's peace offering with a nod. "Just remember, little one, that we all share this jungle," Louie said, his voice gentle.

Next, Milo approached Benny the Bear, who was still looking at his empty fishing net with sad eyes. "I'm sorry, Benny," Milo said, handing him half of the bananas. "I hope we can still be friends." Benny's eyes lit up, and he patted Milo's head. "Of course, Milo. Just don't take what's not yours next time," he chuckled.

Milo continued on, sharing bananas with all the animals he had wronged. With each apology, he felt lighter, and the jungle seemed to brighten around him. He even helped the ants carry a banana slice to their hill, earning a parade of grateful antennae wiggles.

As the stars began to twinkle in the twilight sky, Milo climbed to his favorite branch, looking out over the peaceful jungle. He had returned all the bananas and, in doing so, had found something much sweeter: the joy of doing good.

"Milo the Monkey learned his lesson," he whispered to himself, a contented smile on his face. "And tomorrow is a new day, with no plans for banana bonanzas, but maybe for a new adventure—one that includes all of my friends."

And with that thought, Milo curled up in the crook of the tree, the gentle sounds of the nocturnal jungle lulling him to sleep. He dreamed not of bananas, but of laughter and fun shared with friends, of a jungle filled with happiness and harmony.

Visit us at https://www.YoungMindsPublishing.com for more books and information on upcoming releases.